E
Cu

$8.95

Curious George at the railroad station

DATE DUE			
FE 21 '89	JY 24 '90	AG 01 '91	FE 23 '93
MR 29 '89	AG 14 '90	AG 7 '91	MR 30 '93
AP 24 '89	SE 10 '90	NO 18 '91	MY 13 '93
MY 4 '89	NO 23 '90	DE 16 '91	MY 28 '93
MY 26 '89	JA 31 '91	FE 7 '92	JA 15 '93
JE 20 '89	MR 22 '91	MY 1 '92	JY 22 '93
JY 27 '89	AP 19 '91	JE 30 '92	JA 26 '93
AG 4 '89	MY 8 '91	JY 1 '92	SE 14 '93
AG 29 '89	JE 7 '91	JY 9 '92	SE 28 '93
SE 21 '89	JY 5 '91	JY 23 '92	FEB 7 '94
AP 7 '90	JY 22 '91	AG 17 '92	APR 25 '94
JY 10 '90		NO 6 '92	OCT 14 '94
		DE 17 '92	JAN 26 '95
			FEB 06 '95

Curious George®

AT THE RAILROAD STATION

Adapted from the Curious George film series
edited by Margret Rey and Alan J. Shalleck

1 9 8 8

Houghton Mifflin Company, Boston

Library of Congress Cataloging-in-Publication Data

Curious George visits the railroad station/edited by Margret Rey and
  Alan J. Shalleck.
      p.   cm.
    "Adapted from the Curious George film series."
    Summary: Switching around the numbers and letters on the arrival—
departure board seems harmless to Curious George, but it causes
mass mayhem in the train station.
    ISBN 0-395-48667-X
    [1. Monkeys—Fiction. 2. Railroads—Stations—Fiction.] I. Rey,
Margret. II. Shalleck, Alan J.
PZ7.C92188   1988   88-14741
[E]—dc19   CIP
                          AC

Printed in the United States of America

Y   10   9   8   7   6   5   4   3   2   1

George and the man with the yellow hat
took their friend Mrs. Green to the railroad station.

"George," said the man, "I'll go and help
Mrs. Green with her ticket. Look around,
but don't get into trouble."

George looked around.
He saw a man and his son
on their way to catch a train.

He also saw a trainmaster moving
letters and numbers around on a big sign.

What did the letters and numbers mean?
George was curious.

When the trainmaster climbed down
from the platform,

George climbed up.

He moved a letter, then a number.
What a nice game!

"What's that monkey doing to the schedule?" yelled a man. "Now I don't know when my train leaves!"

George was scared.

He jumped down from the platform.
"Get him!" everyone shouted.

George ran through the crowd, ran past the gate,
and jumped into a waste basket to hide.
Now he was safe.

Nearby, the little boy and his father
were standing in line
waiting for their train.

"All aboard!" shouted the conductor.

"Look, Daddy. There's our train," said the little boy,
and he ran off . . .

... just as the trainmaster was closing the gate.

"Come back, son," the father shouted.
"That's not our train!"
But it was too late.

The boy tried to open the gate, but it was locked.

He began to cry.

George peeked out of the waste basket
and saw the toy engine
starting to roll toward the tracks.

"There goes my engine!" cried the boy,
and he ran after it.

George leaped out of the basket,

ran past the boy, and stopped the toy engine
just before it fell onto the tracks.

The very next moment, a train pulled in.

The trainmaster opened a gate,
and the boy's father ran to his son.

"There you are!" shouted the trainmaster.
"You made a lot of trouble on that big board!"

"Please don't be angry with George," said the father.
"He saved my son."

"Well," said the trainmaster,
"I guess that makes George a hero."

The people on the platform cheered and clapped.
"Hooray for George!"

Just then, the man with the yellow hat came over.
"Come on, George," he said. "Mrs. Green is on
her train, and it's time for the hero to go home."